ON SILVER WINGS

ON SILVER WINGS

SYDNEY WINWARD

On Silver Wings

Cover art by RJ Creatives Graphic Services

Published by Silver Forge Books

Digital ISBN: 978-1-960461-10-0

Paperback: 978-1-960461-11-7

www.sydneywinward.com

To the little fairy in all of us

BOOKS BY SYDNEY WINWARD

The Bloodborn Series
Bloodborn
Bloodbond
Bloodscourge
Bloodbane
Bloodcurse
Bloodheir

Sunlight and Shadows Series
A Breath of Sunlight
A Taste of Shadows
A Glimpse of Music
A Kiss of Embers
A Balm of Healing

Letters to Love Series
Yours, Sterling
Forever, Mirabelle
Always, Ivette
Charles, With Love

Lord Death Series
A Waltz with Lord Death

Novellas
Through Wylder Meadows
Root Brew Float
On Silver Wings
Bloodmoon
Selkie

1

A CHILL RACED UP Gabriel's spine as he waited in the shadows, his back pressed against a pine tree. A frosty breath escaped his mouth, and a river of gooseflesh ran up his arms and pricked the back of his neck. His muscles ached from remaining still for so long, but he had far too much to lose to take a single misstep.

Moonlight glinted off the surface of the snow, thousands of glittering flakes sparkling in the midnight forest. A streak of red stained the fresh powder, only the juice from winter berries, but the smear gave the appearance of blood.

The heat of desperation entered his hands and dispelled the frigid ice trudging through his veins as he glanced toward the sky. The moon shifted on the navy-blue canvas until it hung directly over his head.

His fingers trembled as he produced a thick blade of grass and brought it to his lips. Taking a deep breath, he blew on the grass, and a foul, vibrating screech followed.

His eyebrows furrowed when the tone sounded wrong, so he adjusted the piece of grass and tried again.

Another foul screech escaped, perfectly imitating a wounded rabbit.

He squeezed his eyes shut and prayed for safety from predators like chupacabras or manticores. But he quickly snapped his eyes open again when he heard a faint jingle riding on the breeze.

Without missing a beat in his rabbit distress call, he watched the smear of berries, his eyes aching with the strain. A second jingle carried on the wind like tinkling wind chimes. His heart sped up with nervous anticipation. He had seconds to get this right; otherwise, he'd miss his chance altogether.

A shimmer darted through the clearing, almost too small for his human eyes to follow. It raced past a second time and into a cluster of trees. Just when he thought his target disappeared completely, the shimmer moved out of the trees and toward the smear of red on the snow.

Gabriel moved quickly, picking up his ax and smashing it into the rope hanging in the tree. A net made of fine weaving escaped from its hiding place in the boughs and landed directly on top of the red smear.

All became quiet in the forest.

Please, he begged as he raced toward the trap with a jar in his hands, white powder flying up in his wake. He skidded to a stop in the snow and dropped to his knees.

Only for his heart to drop.

A smear of red berries and white powder lay beneath the net. Nothing more.

He'd failed.

A heavy ache pressed down on his shoulders and crushed his heart. A frigid wind suffocated him, stealing the breath from his lungs. He sat on his heels and gazed up at the moon as two silent tears trailed from the corners of his eyes. Hours of preparation—wasted. He must have cut the rope too soon. Or perhaps the faerie had spotted him in the shadows.

The trickle of tears froze on his face from the exposure to the biting cold. He wanted to weep until nothing but raw emotion remained inside him. He wanted to cry out to the dark skies in anguish over what his failure meant.

The faintest tinkle broke him out of his prison of heartache. His eyes widened as he breathed in sharply. The tinkle sounded again, muffled beneath a mound of snow.

Hope surged within him like spring sunshine breaking through a river of ice. He clambered toward the sound, brushing snow away with his hands until he found her. The four-inch faerie pulsed with silver light as she lay in the snow. Her silvery, translucent wings drooped as if burdened with fatigue.

Although her face was indecipherable in the pulsing light, her body tensed with fright when she noticed him kneeling over her. She scrambled to her feet, but the moment she leaped into the air in an attempt to flee, he scooped her into the jar and shut the lid tight. Only a small hole in the top provided her with the means to breathe.

"Let me out!" she screamed as she pounded on the glass before she pushed on the cork from the bottom. The small faerie wasn't large enough or strong enough to make it budge.

A chilling howl echoed in the woods, sending a shiver down his spine. He quickly retrieved his ax, replaced the leather guard, and tied the weapon to his belt. Hope flared bright within him as he rushed away from the clearing as fast as he dared.

He weaved through pine trees. He trudged through knee-deep snow. And only when he deemed himself far enough from the threat did he slow his pace and lift the jar to better peer at his new captive.

The faerie's light pulsed quickly, undoubtedly with anger. She looked like a small human but with wings, though he could only make out the faintest glimpse of her face.

"Release me," she demanded with hands on her hips, her small voice muffled through the glass.

"I cannot." He handled the jar, careful not to tip it lest she lose her balance and hurt herself. "Tell me, faerie. Are the rumors true? You will grant me any wish I desire as long as I have you in my custody?"

She turned her back to him, her arms crossed as she fluttered her wings. He took the action as an insult. He'd never met a faerie before, but he couldn't help but wonder if they were all stubborn, or just this one.

He sighed and ran a hand through his shoulder-length brown hair, half of it tied back to keep it from falling in his face. "We have a three-day journey ahead of us. I will release you after I receive my wish." He paused and stared at her wings. One drooped a little more than the other, and a flicker of concern ignited within him. "Are you injured?"

The faerie looked at him over her shoulder, and again, he wished he could see her face. Unless she didn't have a face… He wasn't entirely sure what faeries looked like underneath all that pulsing light. She could have blue skin and he'd be none the wiser.

Again, she fluttered her wings, a tinkling sound accompanying the movement. "Your net hit me. What else did you expect?"

"I'm sorry." A guilty grimace pulled his mouth into a frown as he continued trudging through the snow. The moon provided ample light through the forest, but despite his ability to traverse the wild, unbeaten path in the night, an unforgiving chill seeped into his bones. His limbs shivered. His teeth chattered. But he trekked forward and ignored his protesting body. After several minutes of silence, he added, "It was not my intention to injure you. May I have a look? Is there something I can do to help?"

In response, she turned her back to him, her wing drooping even further as if burdened by fatigue. Her light flickered in a fearful rhythm despite her unconcerned facade. Another wave of guilt washed over him, but he batted it aside and focused on his original goal.

Rosamund.

His legs moved faster at the thought of his youngest daughter.

Another howl echoed in the woods, farther than the last he'd heard. He attempted to quicken his pace, but when the jarring movement knocked the faerie to her knees, he stopped.

Uncertainty warred within him as he glanced in the direction of the howl and back to the small creature in the jar. Making camp would be the smartest decision to care for the injured faerie, despite her stubborn, silent protests. Yet, he wanted to put distance between him and whatever lay at the end of those howls.

A chill wind picked up and obscured the path in front of him with a miniature flurry. His stiff fingers struggled to grip the jar, and the tips of his ears had turned to icicles long ago.

The flurry stung his face like hungry vipers, and only then did he shield himself with one arm as he veered to the right through the storm.

A large, rocky face greeted him within minutes, offering a promise of shelter from the elements. He slipped inside a hollow space barely large enough for him to stand. Carefully, he placed the jar down and set his pack aside before he ventured out once more in search of dry kindling. When he returned, the faerie continued to face her back to him, from stubbornness or fear, he wasn't sure.

He continuously glanced toward the mouth of the small cave as he built his fire, watching as a raging storm picked up just outside. An unforgiving wind howled as it rushed past. A blizzard turned the forest backdrop white.

Trying to ignore the haste burning in his gut, he turned his attention to his task. Sparks jumped from the flint and steel in his hands, and within minutes, a soft fire flickered to life, light bouncing across the rocky walls.

Despite his numb fingers, he dug into his pack until he located a purplish salve inside a glass jar. The faerie's wings fluttered lopsidedly when she spotted it, and just for a moment, he glimpsed the silhouette of her face before her light continued to pulse. A defense mechanism?

"I assure you, I mean no harm," he said as he knelt beside her jar. "Allow me to help. I—"

"Stay away from me," she hissed as she backed up as far as the jar allowed.

His hands froze as he gazed down at her fearful stance. She wasn't just afraid—she was terrified. He couldn't blame her. If he were in her shoes, he was sure he'd be terrified, too. Guilt churned in his gut, but the reminder of Rosamund kept him grounded. Unfortunately, the ends justified the means.

He stretched out beside the fire and watched the storm rage on.

Hold on, Rosamund. I'm coming.

LORELLA'S HEART BEAT unbearably fast, and with it, the power within her flickered in response to her fear. Her magical aura pulsed like a frightened songbird in flight. Although she knew she could usually use magic to escape this glass prison, she was also overly aware of the fetters that bound her power in captivity.

She swallowed the lump in her throat as she kept her gaze down, not daring to look the man in the eyes. Getting captured by a human was usually a death sentence for her kind. They wanted more and more and more until faeries had nothing left to give.

An aching pain flared in her upper back where her muscles refused to lift her injured wing. The net had come out of nowhere and wouldn't have trapped her if she'd realized the red snow was berries and not blood. But she'd realized too late, only a half second away to freedom.

Her muscles screamed in protest as she tried once again to flutter her wings. The action only seemed to injure them further.

A sob came unbidden to her throat, but when the human snapped his attention in her direction, she clamped her mouth shut and endured the pain.

"Are you cold?" he asked softly. "Hungry? What will make you more comfortable?"

"Release me," she demanded in a shaky tone.

The man sighed and hung his head. "I cannot. Not yet at least."

That's what they always say.

Shivers ran through her as she thought of one of her friends. Her captor had squeezed every last drop of magic from her. She hadn't survived the strain on her weakened body.

"I need to escape," she whispered to herself so he wouldn't hear. "But how?"

The magical thread that forced her into servitude tied her down after capture, and it would not release her until the man let her go of his own free will.

After a few minutes, the human leaned back against the cave wall and closed his eyes. Sleep seemed to take him immediately, as if every bone inside him was exhausted to the core. His chest slowly rose and fell with each deep breath, and the tension in his shoulders relaxed.

Her gaze ran over his sleeping face as she studied him for the first time since her capture. Brown stubble ran across his jaw. Tendrils of brown hair brushed his shoulders. His muscular arms flexed as he gripped the handle of his ax in his sleep. He couldn't have been more than thirty years old, and he certainly was handsome for a human.

Unfortunately, he would no sooner take her life in his quest for riches and renown than release her from undeserving captivity.

Lorella sank to her knees in defeat. The only way to escape captivity and the magic fetters tying her to this man was for him to either release her or die.

The burning heat of anguish lit beneath her knees. What if she never saw her family again? Her friends? What if she never again experienced the freedom of flight in the midnight skies?

Her anguish burned hotter and hotter, but then she gasped as the heat seared her skin. She jumped to her feet, her eyes wide, when she realized the glass jar lay too close to the fire. It wasn't anguish at all, but blazing heat.

Within seconds, the small space inside the jar became scorching like an unforgiving summer drought. She bounced from one foot to the other, her dainty slippers the only things keeping her feet from harm.

Her wings drooped. Beads of perspiration lined her brow. She dove deep within herself for her pool of magic but stopped short when a steel gate blocked her from entering.

Dread snapped her back to reality as she stared at the crackling fire. She was bound to her master—she could not use magic without his permission.

The flames burned brighter as they fed on the kindling, and with it, the heat transferred to the glass jar. Panic consumed her when the temperature increased. With the intention of tipping the jar and breaking it, she slammed her shoulder into the translucent wall, only to gasp when the hot surface burned her.

She jumped upward and latched onto the bottom of the cork, only barely managing to grip the spongy surface. There was not enough space to transform into her larger faerie form.

The stifling atmosphere quickly became unbearably hot, her wings drooping even further. Panic encouraged her to do the one thing she never thought she'd do.

"Human!" she screeched.

He bolted upright and staggered to his feet, his ax in his hand. His bleary eyes traveled over the space of the cave until he spotted her. "What is it?"

"The jar is hot," she wheezed, clutching tighter onto the cork while her wings dangled uselessly beneath her. "Let me out!"

The man gave no pause as he stumbled toward her. He hissed as he touched the jar, but the heat didn't stop him from uncorking the bottle. The moment she breathed in fresh, cool air, she dropped to the ground and darted into a small crevice in the rock face.

Heavy breaths filled her lungs as she struggled to regain the ability to breathe correctly. Out of all the scenarios she'd imagined over the past hour about her death, dying in a blazing inferno of a jar was not one of them.

"I'm so sorry," the man said. "I didn't realize… I didn't mean to… Are you alright?"

Taking another deep breath, she leaned back against the frigid rock surface and sighed in relief. The coolness seeped into her body, helping to restore the damage done. However, her wings ached, and no matter how hard she tried, she couldn't lift them at all anymore.

"I am an ice faerie," she murmured. "Extreme heat is damaging to us. I fear my wings…"

She couldn't finish her sentence when a sob lodged in her throat. What if she could never fly again?

His footsteps echoed away from her and returned a few moments later, followed by a *whoosh*. Her mouth fell open in surprise when he dumped a pile of snow near her and then moved away.

The light from her aura flickered to obscure her as she poked her head around the corner. Although he watched her, he made no move to approach. She hesitantly took one step and then another until she dove into the snow and covered herself in its cool relief.

Strength returned slowly to her wings, but despite the frost providing them with a cool barrier, they remained limp. She needed her magic to help restore them. But as a prisoner, she had none she could take for herself.

"I'm sorry," he said again, sincerity in his tone. "I truly did not mean to injure you."

But you have. Twice.

When the snow wasn't enough, she picked herself up and ambled toward the entrance of the cave.

"Wait. Don't leave. Please." Even as he said it, he stood in her path as if he readied himself to catch her if she attempted to take flight.

She sighed and despondently shook her head. "Faeries are bound to their masters until released. I cannot go if I wanted to."

After a pause, he let her pass, his eyebrows drawn with concern.

A blast of cold, blizzardy air hit her face, providing instant relief for her drooping wings. She sat in a pile of snow and closed her eyes, lifting her head to the tempest. Even more strength returned to her. But once again, it wasn't enough. She tried her hardest not to dwell on what would happen if her wings didn't heal.

Rocks scraped beside her, followed by a quiet exhale. Although he didn't join her outside in the blizzard, he sat just within the protection of the cave, only several paces away.

"Tell me your name." His gaze fixed on her, and for the first time since her capture, she allowed herself to look into his eyes. A kind soul stared back at her. Kind. Desperate. Determined.

Her light pulsed slower as she dared to stand and attempt to stretch her wings. Pain stabbed her back at her effort. The man shifted where he sat but made no attempt to snatch her. He simply watched.

"Lorella," she answered.

"I'm Gabriel."

A frown formed on her face. Humans weren't benevolent unless they wanted something from her kind. "What is your wish?" she asked, getting straight to the point. She could not delay the inevitable for long. Although she was still wary, she no longer feared for her life. The human didn't seem intent on hurting her, despite having done so by accident.

Gabriel's eyebrows furrowed together, worry setting in the small creases in his forehead. "My daughter is ill. I fear she won't last until the end of the week."

"Where is your daughter? With your wife?"

He shook his head. "My wife passed away several years ago. My eldest of the two, Elaine, is watching over Rosamund."

Her heart skipped in surprise. He wasn't after riches or renown. Rather, his quest was a worthy endeavor. Could it be possible he truly would release her, after all?

Her frown matched his own. Humans were never satisfied after one magical gift.

"And you want me to heal her?"

"Yes."

She looked out into the white blizzard and murmured, "Great is the man who extends a friendly hand. Sorrowful is the man who tightens the band."

"I don't understand."

"Mankind never does. Friends of faeries are gifted favors. Those who capture our kind demand more and more until we are forced to give our last drop of magic." She gazed into his eyes, though she suspected he couldn't see her as well as she could him through her aura of light. "Tell me, Gabriel, will you be satisfied after your daughter is healed? Will you release me then?"

"Of course."

She paused and looked him over, her mouth pursed with doubt. "We'll see."

"What happens when you give all your magic?"

"I die."

The creases on his forehead deepened as his gaze darted to her wings. "One favor. No more. I promise."

"You would not give me a choice?"

He sighed and shook his head, averting his gaze. "I can't risk it. I can't lose my little girl."

But I am expendable.

However, she didn't say it out loud.

"Then if it is within my power, I will grant your wish."

Neither said another word as the blizzard raged harder, its howls drowning out even her thoughts. The longer the haphazard snow decreased visibility of the way ahead, the better. Because it gave her more time to think. And she needed all the time she could get.

A long, piercing howl jolted Gabriel awake. His eyes flew open, and he scrambled for his ax in the dim light of early morning. Smoke from the dwindling fire entered his nose and burned his bleary eyes.

Chills raced up his spine when another howl ripped through the skies. Dread thickened the air as he gazed out at the expanse of snow, no longer burdened by an unrelentless snowstorm. That wasn't a wolf howl. That belonged to a chupacabra.

"Lorella," he called out quietly, afraid anything more than a whisper might attract the dangerous beasts to their campsite. When she didn't answer, he scanned the snow near the cave, only to find her missing.

For a moment, despair washed over him when he thought she might have left, but then he spotted a pulsing light on a low-hanging branch of a nearby tree. His despair turned into discomfort. Had she heard the howls? She was either asleep or didn't seem concerned.

He returned to the cave to gather his belongings, taking heart that he didn't hear the howl again. Snow crunched beneath his boots as he made his way toward the faerie, his movements as slow and silent as possible.

Lorella's light pulsed steadily where her small body lay across the branch, her face almost visible in the serene stillness of sleep. Guilt smashed into him when he noticed her drooping wings. He hadn't meant to injure her. If she would only allow him close enough, he knew his salve could help.

Halfway to the tree, a menacing growl stopped him in his tracks. His heart jumped to his throat as he spun toward the sound, only for it to drop into his stomach. Three black chupacabras stalked toward him on lithe feet, fangs bared. The spikes on their backs stiffened, making them appear bigger and more formidable.

He raised his ax, but the small protection did nothing to soothe his fears.

"Stay back!" He swung his weapon through the air, and although the beasts eyed it, they branched off from one another to surround him instead of ceasing their advancement.

Panic urged his heartbeat into a frenzy as he spun every which way, attempting to keep his eye on all three at once. Their eyes glowed red in the dim morning light, hungry for blood.

A flutter of wings caught his attention, and when he glanced up for a brief moment to find Lorella climbing to her feet on the branch, one of the beasts lunged.

Sharp teeth dug into his arm, and he cried out as he attempted to wrench himself free from its mighty grip. Fiery pain burst through his arm, blood soaking into his sleeve. He slammed his ax down onto the creature, its teeth dislodging from his skin as it became limp.

The other two chupacabras attacked, and he only managed to lodge his weapon into one of the beasts while the other jumped onto his back.

A scream erupted from his mouth as fangs sank into his shoulder. He reached behind him in an attempt to throw the chupacabra off him, but it dug its fangs in deeper and latched onto his back with its sharp claws.

His legs collapsed when a sudden weakness overcame him as the creature sucked his blood. Black dots danced at the corners of his vision. White snow turned crimson.

Breath slowly leaked from his lungs, his limbs too weak to fight off the beast.

He was going to die. He had failed his daughter.

Lorella watched with wide, fearful eyes as the chupacabra feasted on the human's blood. She stood frozen to the spot as uncertainty flickered within her. If she allowed him to die, she would be free. But if she helped him, she risked being bound for the rest of her likely short life.

She balled her hands into fists, her eyebrows furrowing together with determination. No matter what happened to her, she could not stand idle while another person suffered.

With one graceful movement, she launched herself from the branch and transformed into her larger faerie form. Her magic refused to obey her just like it had earlier in the cave, but when she pushed the chupacabra off Gabriel, it rolled several times in the snow and lay still in a daze. She stood protectively in front of the human, her arms outstretched to make herself appear larger. The chupacabra stared back at her, blood dripping from its mouth. It made no attempt to attack again, but rather gazed back at her with a deep sadness in its eyes.

It was a sadness she understood all too well.

THE BURNING PAIN in Gabriel's back and shoulder disappeared in a moment of distracted surprise. His mouth fell open, his eyes wide as he gazed at what appeared to be an angel. A beautiful, otherworldly angel.

Iridescent gossamer wings dripped down her back that sparkled beneath early morning's dim light. A shimmer lined her silvery eyes, dusted her petal-pink lips, and traveled down her neck and to her bare shoulders. A gown seemingly crafted from starlight hugged her curves and blended in with her wings. Her white-blonde hair was pulled up in an elegant updo, several strands brushing against her shoulders.

Her voice broke him out of his trance, and fiery pain crashed back into him in a burst of agony.

"You will return to your burrow," she said in a light, airy voice. "You will not bother this human any longer." The chupacabra whined and bowed its head in submission.

She lowered her arms and approached the beast slowly. Gabriel struggled to move as his entire body hurt, pain pulsing through him with each movement. His fingers managed to graze his weapon hidden in the confines of the snow, but he paused when she crouched and placed a kiss on top of the beast's head. A shimmery imprint lingered after she pulled away, only to seep into its fur moments later and disappear.

The chupacabra spun on its heel and bounded away.

Gabriel grunted, his teeth clenched as he endured the agony of sitting. She spun to face him, and the moment their gazes locked, it felt as if he tumbled backward into a pool of starlight. His heart raced and filled with warmth of the likes he hadn't felt in a very long time.

It was as if he were struck dumb when in the presence of an ethereal beauty, of a woman who could have fallen to earth from the heavens as a radiant star.

One word described her—breathtaking.

He'd heard plenty of stories about faeries, that a single glimpse could bring a full-grown man to his knees. Of course, he'd thought it ridiculous at the time. But now? It didn't seem quite so ridiculous anymore.

"You are the faerie?" he asked in a breathless whisper.

"This is my larger form, yes."

"You are…you are…*beautiful.*" The description hardly did her justice, especially when the moonlight bathed her form in an otherworldly radiance.

Her cheeks dusted pink. "Thank you."

Another wave of burning agony ripped through his back. He gritted his teeth as the pain pulsed through him. Blood continued to stain the snow red, telling him his wound was deep enough to kill him. He was going to die if he didn't do something.

Unless…

He glanced toward Lorella and opened his mouth to speak, but the moment her slender fingers touched his arm, his words fled him. Warmth traveled through his veins, his stomach tying in knots despite the horrendous pain in his back. She was so close. Only a few breaths away.

Her fingers moved from his arm and touched his chest, just over his heart. "I should have acted sooner. You've lost too much blood. Your essence is fading."

Black shadows crept into the corners of his vision, but he blinked them back, if only to gaze at Lorella for a few moments longer.

"Can you help?" he asked, his words slurred as foggy confusion muddled his thoughts. He placed his hand over hers. A tingle traveled up his arm at the simple touch. "Heal me. Please. With your magic."

Instantaneously, Lorella frowned and retracted her hand. "Is it your command?"

"Yes."

A sliver of guilt touched his conscience, but he didn't dwell on it for long when both his and Rosamund's lives hung in the balance. He needed to return to her, or all would be for naught.

"Very well."

Her fingers glowed with silver light as she placed one hand on his forehead and the other over his heart. Her power flowed into him. Soothing. Gentle. Relieving.

As the seconds passed, the pain in his back and shoulder lessened, and his strength returned. But when she released him, she swayed on unsteady feet, only to catch herself on the trunk of a tree. Her face looked a shade paler than before. Her wings drooped further as if the strength to lift them was far too much of a burden to bear.

He rolled his shoulder, buoyed by the fact that it no longer hurt. Rather, his body felt stronger than before.

Not wanting to dwell further on it only to lose precious time, he picked up his ax and returned it to his belt. His gaze passed over the blood-soaked snow, and he grimaced to see just how much blood he'd lost.

Too much.

"If we hurry, we can reach my town in two days, maybe less."

Determination clung to each step he took across the snowy landscape, his daughter's face filling his mind. He'd been alone for so long, struggling to straddle the line between caretaker and provider. If Rosamund died…

His stomach twisted at the thought. He'd never forgive himself if he lost her. If he'd only been a better father. If he'd only taken her to the physician when her symptoms had just started. If he'd only been wealthier to afford the care she needed.

The sun began to rise in a beautiful collage of yellow and orange. A soft pink weaved onto the breathtaking canvas, spreading a faint blush across the forest.

He glanced over his shoulder, only for alarm to flit across his face. Lorella's wings drooped so much that they dragged in the snow behind her, creating a trail of exhaustion in her wake. This journey was not going as expected. And she was the one suffering for it.

"Lorella," he said softly.

Her eyes opened a fraction more as she stopped at the sound of her name. However, when he reached out for her, she flinched away.

Instead of trying again, he dug into his pack and pulled out the jar of salve. "I thought I would need it for myself, but you need it more than I do." What a fool he was for using her magic to heal him rather than trying this first. He hadn't been thinking straight at the time. "Will you allow me?" He gestured to her wings.

The faerie's gaze hardened with caution as she studied the jar. "What is a human doing with a magical remedy?"

He grimaced as he considered lying about his long-kept secret. But he knew she would see right through him if she already guessed at the magical properties of the salve. "My wife was a witch. It seems my eldest, Elaine, has developed some of her mother's talents."

If she was surprised, she didn't show it. "Then why not have Elaine heal Rosamund?"

"We've tried everything we could think of. Nothing has worked. Faerie magic is stronger." He took another step forward, and she took a half-step back. "This will help your wings."

The silver of her eyes shimmered with distrust. "Humans don't help faeries."

"Then you've never met a decent human."

Uncertainty stared back at him as she seemed to contemplate his offer, but finally, her shoulders relaxed. "Fine. But leave your weapons over there." She pointed to a tree ten paces away.

"Do you think I'd hurt you?"

"What do you think some humans do to faeries to make sure they don't escape?"

He took one glance at her wings, then at his weapon, and frowned. "I would never do something so cruel." In fact, his stomach churned at the thought of anyone doing something so terrible to a faerie. He felt awful enough for damaging her wings from his net and then from the heat of the jar.

He did as instructed, and even pulled out a small knife from his pocket, leaning both the knife and his ax against the trunk of the tree. When he returned, her shoulders stiffened again as if uncomfortable with the idea of him touching her.

A warning flashed in his mind, an urge to keep moving to reach his daughter quicker, but he could not continue his journey while Lorella suffered. It would take only a few minutes. No more.

Gingerly, she perched on a boulder and turned her body to expose her wings to him. His breath caught—not from awe this time but from shock. Her right wing was torn in several places. A big, purple bruise lay in the spot where skin connected with wing.

He'd done this to her… All he'd wanted was to capture a faerie. He'd never meant to hurt her. But now he felt an intense desire to help her, to provide the same relief she'd given him earlier.

"Tell me about your family," he murmured in an attempt to keep her distracted. He unstopped the bottle of salve and scooped a portion of the purple substance out with his fingers. "Brothers? Sisters? Husband? Children?"

A muffled grunt escaped her as he applied the salve to her back as gently as possible. It shimmered as the magic took effect, and the wound began to heal, if only slightly. At the very least, it should provide relief from the pain.

For a moment, he thought she might not answer his intrusive question, but then she said, "Two sisters. A brother. I am not married, though my sister, Cassia, often teases that I am married to the moon."

She cracked a smile. A real, genuine, heart-stopping smile. His heart beat faster in his chest, heat pulsing through his veins as he couldn't help but stare. She was beautiful. A mountain of mystery shrouded her, and he wanted to learn more.

"You seem comfortable in the night," he commented. His fingers hovered over her wings for a moment as he hesitated. Touching her wings seemed far too intimate, and he also feared being too rough with them.

He skimmed the tip of his finger over the worst of the tears, but quickly snapped his hand back when she whimpered. "Does it hurt?"

Instead of answering, she simply nodded.

"Bear with me. It shouldn't hurt for much longer."

When he spread the salve across her wing, her body shivered with pain, but she still spoke through gritted teeth. "I am nocturnal. I am more comfortable at night than during the day. There is a stillness you don't usually experience when the sun is out."

"The night certainly is beautiful," he said as he started on another tear. "May I ask a question?"

A moment of hesitation passed before she nodded.

"How did you tame the chupacabra? And why did you kiss it?"

She gave him a sideways glance. The moment their eyes locked, his heart resumed its frenzy. "Faerie folk arc friends with all creatures alike. The chupacabra respected me, and I him. I don't blame you for killing his family. You did what you had to do to save yourself." She grimaced again as he continued his administration, but after a moment of healing, she continued, "Those who are kissed by a faerie are blessed."

His gaze darted to her shimmering pink lips. His mind must have been muddled by the beast attack because a sudden desire to find out what her kisses tasted like took a hold of him.

He squeezed his eyes shut for several seconds to center himself.

"And you, human? How old are your daughters?"

The last of the salve ran out after he used it on a perpendicular tear near the tip of her wing. The membrane slowly knitted together beneath the witch remedy, and the pain in her expression smoothed out to relief. "Elaine is nine. Rosamund is five. They've both had to do a lot of growing up in the last five years after their mother passed away. And please, call me Gabriel."

"Gabriel." His name on her tongue sent a delightful shiver down his spine. He squeezed his eyes shut again.

Surely, this sudden desire had something to do with faerie magic.

But when she smiled at him, he realized that wasn't the case when his stomach tied in knots. There was something about her, as if their souls were no strangers.

He wondered if she felt it, too.

He chastised himself for the thought. Of course not. She'd made it clear she feared humans, and he hadn't done much to prove her wrong, either.

The magic in the purple salve glistened like sunlight on the ocean, and she held still as she allowed it to heal her. Gently, he touched her wing to inspect it. The thin, gossamer membrane finished knitting back together, much to his relief.

A tense silence crept between them, one charged with energy and longing. At least on his end. "I never thanked you for saving my life," he murmured, suddenly realizing how callous he'd been by not thanking her sooner. "I appreciate what you did back there." His fingers shifted from her wing to brush the soft, delicate skin of her shoulder.

She snapped her attention to him as if startled, though she didn't move.

"Sorry." He grimaced as he let his hand drop. "How are your wings feeling?"

"Better," she answered hesitantly while staring back at him. Energy continued to swirl between them, pulsing alive as they gazed at one another. The sound of her voice cut through the thick tension. "You are not like most other humans I've come across. Your aura is…different."

"My aura?" He wasn't sure if he should accept a compliment or frown at an insult.

The light of dawn glimmered against her skin, once again stealing the breath from his lungs at the mesmerizing beauty. "A good different. I'm not sure what to make of you."

They gazed back at each other for another several moments before a flush crept up his neck. He cleared his throat and broke eye contact with her as if severing a spell. "Let's keep moving."

A heavy weight pulled on his eyelids, begging him to stop and rest. But every moment he wasted meant another second Rosamund was closer to meeting Death.

A shudder ran through his body. He gathered his weapons and started the journey south with the light of day to guide him. Lorella trailed him again, but this time instead of following at a distance, she kept pace with him only a few steps behind. As the hours passed, her drooping wings stiffened as healing and strength returned to them. He had planned to save the salve for himself should he need it, but he couldn't let her suffer.

A pit of guilt dropped in his stomach, but he kept his eyes forward, his resolve unwavering. He would release her as soon as his daughter was healed.

Conversation helped to ease his worries for his daughter's welfare. And the longer they conversed, the more Lorella's guarded wall seemed to fall in his presence. However, he knew the wall was still there, and he also worried she might find a way to leave when he needed her most.

When the sun began its descent over the course of the short winter day, he glanced over his shoulder to find the faerie watching him again with a tilt to her head. Studying him. Almost as if she were still trying to figure him out.

"We should stop to rest," she said. "You look as if you're about to drop."

"I can't. My daughter—"

"—will be worse off if you collapse from exhaustion. Even I can tell you've hardly slept in days."

Yes, she was right. But…

His gaze traveled toward the horizon slowly transitioning from blue to an orange and pink mixture. Gray clouds hovered in the distance as if warning of an oncoming storm. A chill swept into the air, spinning a flurry of snow around his ankles. But otherwise, the dusk was calm and quiet, unlike earlier when they'd faced a storm and chupacabras.

"Come on," Lorella murmured, startling him when she touched his arm.

He sharply turned his head to catch the mesmerizing shimmer in her silver eyes. For a moment, he wished to give her anything she wanted, if only to once again witness her smile stretched across her face.

"We rest for only one more night," he relented with a sigh. "And then we arrive tomorrow."

Together, they traveled off the snow-packed path and traversed through a thicket of bushes before settling down in a small clearing shadowed by trees near a frozen lake. The sunset sky glimmered off the ice like jewels sparking beneath sunlight.

For a moment, he hesitated, glancing uncertainly at Lorella as he held several bundles of dry wood in his arms. The last time he'd created a fire, it had nearly killed her. But he wouldn't survive the night without warmth.

As if attuned to his thoughts, she said, "I can handle being beside a fire for a time." The corner of her mouth twitched in amusement. "Just not trapped inside a jar next to the flames."

Setting the bundle of wood down, he buried his face in his hands at the reminder of his blunder. He had to let her go. He couldn't do this to her.

But then what? Watch as his daughter was taken by the fever?

"Gabriel—"

"I need to hunt for game," he interrupted quickly as he stepped away from her raised hand, almost as if she were about to touch him. "If you need help, call for me. I won't stray far."

He didn't give her a chance to reply as he stalked out of the clearing and followed a small path leading toward the frozen lake. Hunting for pheasant or rabbit might take him too far away from Lorella, and he wanted to be near enough to protect her if necessary.

Therefore, he gingerly stepped onto the ice, fighting against the pull of gravity as he slid and slipped and struggled to stay on his own two feet. He attempted to clear his mind of everything but his immediate task as he searched for a good spot to fish.

When he found it, he drove his ax downward, chipping into the ice little by little. Once. Twice. And after several more times, the ice cracked into a small fissure. A fish tail thrashed languidly, and his arm darted beneath the surface of the excruciatingly chilly water, grabbed the creature through the mouth and gills, and hefted it out of the water before tossing it onto the ice. The fish flopped the smallest bit, its body clearly too cold to offer much movement.

However, when Gabriel carefully watched for another fish, something lobbed him in the back, and white powder exploded against his shoulder and into his face.

He gasped and spluttered in surprise as his gaze darted toward the source of the attack.

To his shock, Lorella stood at the edge of the lake with a mischievous smile on her face as she tossed another snowball into the air and caught it deftly in one hand.

Without warning, she lobbed that one as well. In his haste to avoid it, he slipped on the ice, crying out as he crashed onto his side.

The snowball still managed to explode across his chest.

"Gabriel!" she called. And with an expert maneuver, she slid across the ice until she came to his side. But when she stooped to take his arm and tried to help him up, she slipped, too, and fell on top of him.

"Oof!" The surprise of her sudden weight knocked the remaining air from his lungs.

Her silver eyes shot wide open as she braced herself against his chest and bolted upright. The shock in her expression was enough to kick down his barriers, and he couldn't help but release loud, hearty laughter, his first glimpse of happiness in who knew how long.

Before she had a chance to react, he scooped up the powdery snow from his chest and shoved it into her face. Now it was her turn to gasp and splutter. But then a wide, mischievous grin spread across her face as she leaped to her feet and effortlessly glided away from him on the ice.

He attempted to follow after but ended up fighting for balance with each uncoordinated step. His feet slipped, and he would have splatted forward if not for him bending over and bracing his hands against the cool surface.

Again, he attempted to move forward, but with only a couple steps, he careened backward and fell once more.

"How do you traverse the ice so well?" he laughed, shaking his head at her as she spun in a circle as if she were on land rather than on a slippery surface.

"I've had a lot of practice." She glided back toward him and took both his hands. "Here. Let me show you how I do it."

The gentleness of her touch sparked a raging heat in his body, starting from the tips of his fingers, down his arms, and straight into his chest as an arrow of infatuation. He shouldn't like Lorella like that. Especially considering their predicament and rough start. But he just couldn't help himself when she had the most captivatingly beautiful silver eyes and the most enticing pink, shimmery lips.

She was kind and thoughtful and showed him a playful, spontaneous side that he adored.

His heart fell for a fraction of a second when he realized this couldn't last. They would soon part ways, and he would never see her again. But for now… He had no qualms about allowing her to teach him more finesse on the ice.

"I'm not so sure I was built for grace," he jested.

In response, she squeezed his fingers. "That doesn't mean you can't still have a bit of fun."

Slowly, she propelled them backward with a flit of her wings. Even the small movement caused him to lose his balance, and he nearly fell again but managed to catch himself with a twist of his body.

After a few more moments, he grew the slightest bit more confident and allowed her to guide them closer to the middle of the small, frozen lake. The light of dusk caught on silver wings as she flitted them gently, quietly, propelling them at a slow pace across the ice.

He laughed in delight when momentarily, his heart felt as light as a cloud as all his worries and cares washed away. At least for a time.

In response, Lorella gave him a dazzling smile that twisted his insides into beautiful knots, filling him with a joy he'd missed out on for the longest time. Over the past five years, he'd worked himself to the bone trying to be the caring father his children had needed. In the process, he hadn't realized he'd lost himself.

He used to laugh a lot more. He used to tease and jest and sing. Until now, he hadn't realized he'd lost all of that.

But it wasn't too late to get them back. He could have happiness and warmth again, laughter and song. Lorella was showing him it was possible to know joy again. With her, he was blissfully happy.

If only for this moment.

"Do you skate on the ice often?" he asked as she maneuvered them back toward the shoreline. "You're a natural."

"My siblings and I skate all the time. There's a pond back home. It's only a fraction of the size of this one, so we skate on it in our smaller faerie forms."

He was reluctant to release her, but he knew he must as he dropped her hands, retrieved his fish, and led the way back to the clearing to set up the fire. "Do you spend more time in your smaller or larger form?"

He pushed over a dead tree leaning precariously against another, and it thumped to the ground, offering Lorella a place to sit while he occupied himself with building the fire and fileting the fish.

Another smile graced her beautiful lips as she leaned forward on her knees. "I'm mostly in my smaller form. I live in a little wooden house tucked within the branches of the same tree as my family. There's safety in numbers. Though, I can't say we haven't been targeted by birds or frogs when we look like insects to them."

"How many of you are there?"

"In my colony? Several hundred of us." Her eyes took on a sudden warmth as she gazed into the fire. "Most of us are active at night and sleep during the day. My favorite thing to do is watch the night sky and the stars that change and shift with the movement of the moon."

"That sounds peaceful."

"It is."

Uncertainty reared its head within him, especially because there seemed to have been a shift between them. A lightheartedness. Perhaps a bit of trust.

But he decided to take his chance, anyway. "I admit I haven't paused long enough to study the night sky. Will you show it to me?"

Instead of rejecting him or pushing him away, a gleam lit up her eyes as she nodded enthusiastically. "I would love to."

They conversed more as they warmed their hands as he ate cooked fish and she winter berries, and when the sky became dark like drapes that had closed over the rest of the world, they lay side by side on the soft foliage Lorella had gathered. Together, they gazed up at the stars.

She explained to him the constellations high above them, tracing each one with the path of one of her slender fingers. Although he didn't quite follow everything she said, he enjoyed the sound of her light, airy voice and feeling her solid presence beside him.

And for just this moment…

They were both happy.

4

A COMFORTING HEAT seeped into Lorella's cheek as she awoke from a deep, peaceful slumber. Slowly, her eyelids fluttered open.

But then she froze when she realized *whose* heat provided such comfort.

Her breath hitched, her eyes snapping wide open when she found her head on Gabriel's shoulder, his hand lightly resting against her waist. His sage-like scent filled her nostrils with each shallow breath. But rather than making her want to flee with the unexpected intimacy of their position, she shocked herself by wanting to draw even closer. To feel his heat on more than just her cheek. To feel the gentle strength of his hands holding her close.

She bolted upright in her confusion, the longing of her thoughts startling her to her feet. Never in her life had she imagined herself falling for a *human*. A faerie, yes. Maybe even a forest elf. But never a human. She'd always thought them reckless and heartless.

Until she'd met Gabriel…

True, as a captured faerie, her bonds still prevented her from claiming her freedom. But where would she go if she found it again? Back home? Because the thought of returning to the forest filled her with aching sadness rather than joyful longing.

She didn't want to return home. She wanted to stay with Gabriel a little longer. Even if their situation was less than ideal.

"You sleep well?" Gabriel croaked, his voice groggy. But by the shift of his gaze from her to the place beside him, she realized he was aware of their intimate position during the night.

"Yes," she said, the smallest flicker of a smile on her lips as she turned her back to him and smoothed her hair. "Yes, I did."

Her cheeks flamed where his warmth still seemed to seep into her. She kept her back turned to him as he kicked snow onto the ashes from the fire and packed up his things. And then her fluster only continued to grow when she felt him only a small step away, near enough to touch.

"Let's get going then. We're almost there."

She released a shaky breath and dared to glance over her shoulder to meet the lovely green and brown hue of his eyes. Unlike when they'd first met, his eyes were now filled with light and hope, and she treasured the way her heart responded with leaps and flutters. No, she couldn't fathom leaving him now. She wanted to see this through, if only to witness his smile at least one last time after she healed Rosamund of her illness.

"Lead the way."

"It's just past the bridge," Gabriel said, pointing to a rope bridge strewn across a wide chasm, "and then a short distance through the forest. We live on the outskirts of town."

He eyed the ropes fluttering with the light morning breeze and the wooden planks spaced evenly apart. He'd forbidden his daughters from crossing it in fear of either of them falling. Instead, whenever they ventured out of town, they took the long way to avoid the chasm.

A lump of dread formed in his throat as he placed his foot on the first wooden plank to test his weight. The ropes groaned in protest, but it held.

Shifting his body slightly, he offered his hand to Lorella. She slid her fingers into his, and the moment their eyes met, he tumbled into a pool of delicate silver. He didn't know who moved first, only that they found themselves only a breath away from the other. The pink shimmer of her lips begged to be kissed.

Their souls seemed to conjoin like long-lost friends, and for a moment, the rational part of his mind stopped working. His hand slid to her waist, and his fingers dared to graze the ends of her soft, blonde hair. Her palm rested against his chest, and he didn't doubt she could feel the way his heart raced at her gentle touch. He couldn't remember the last time he'd been touched by a woman.

"Gabriel," she whispered, and just the sound of his name snapped him out of his daze.

Instead of kissing her like he so desperately wanted, he cleared his throat and stepped away. As she had said earlier, being kissed by a faerie was a gift. He would not steal that gift like he'd temporarily stolen her freedom.

Still holding her hand, he pulled her along behind him as he carefully stepped on one wooden plank and then another. Each piece of weather-damaged wood groaned louder than the last.

The breath shuddered in his lungs, a sweat breaking out across his forehead as he eyed the end of the bridge. It taunted him with the promise of safety. Jagged ice dripped from the cliff's edge, ominous and foreboding. He grimaced at the thought of what might reside in the chasm below—

A yelp escaped him when the wooden plank beneath his foot snapped in half, and his entire leg fell through. He barely caught himself on the plank in front of him rather than slipping farther into the darkness.

Roar!

Gabriel froze, his eyes wide as the beastly bellow echoed off the chasm walls. Involuntarily, his gaze snapped to the dark depths below. Ice climbed through his veins, making his heart work harder to pump blood through his body. His pulse pounded in his ears. A chill squeezed his heart. Something moved in the darkness below, a shadow of a creature. Large. Furry.

And it climbed the icy walls with ease.

Another roar shook the skies—closer this time—moments before the beast jumped high in the air and landed on the bridge behind them.

A troll.

Wood splintered. Ropes shook. Lorella shrieked as the jarring impact nearly threw her over the side of the bridge.

"Go!" he cried, awkwardly shoving her forward after she righted herself when half his body remained wedged between two planks. Thankfully, she heeded his warning as thundering, furry fists struck up a pounding gait in his direction.

Panic consumed him as he tugged and pulled and yanked at his leg. But his trousers were caught on splintered wood and refused to come free.

He dared to glance over his shoulder and wished he hadn't when he spotted the troll's large, underbite tusks, drool dripping from its mouth, and its yellow eyes crazed for his blood.

He tugged harder, but most of his energy went into maintaining his balance as the bridge swayed wildly as if caught in a tempest.

Just as the snarling beast charged the remaining distance, time seemed to move more slowly. Lorella screamed. The troll opened its jaws. And Gabriel slipped the sheath off his ax and plunged it into the beast's neck.

He managed to rip the weapon free just as the troll roared and stumbled backward, shaking the bridge once again. Rather than attempting to yank his leg free, he hacked away at rope after rope. One of them snapped and flung him sideways until he hung upside down. The troll remained upright, furious now more than ever.

His hair hanging wildly from his head, he blindly hacked at the ropes above him as they began shaking with the troll's movement. His arm burned with the effort. His head pounded when far too much blood rushed to it at the awkward angle.

The rope snapped.

An icy, rocky wall slammed into his back. Pain shot from his temples to his foot. Dizziness spun his head every which way, and after a few moments, he gasped in a lungful of air. The troll clung onto his leg, stretching it to the limit until he cried out at the agony. The beast's large, sharp fingernails dug into his foot and then his leg as it climbed.

With one hand clinging to a broken shaft of wood, he used his free hand to swipe at the troll with his ax. The weapon grazed fur on the first swing, and on the second, it sliced the creature's arm. A deafening roar echoed through the chasm.

But it kept climbing.

"Lorella!" he shouted, though he didn't know what he was asking.

Help me.

Flee.

Say goodbye to my daughters for me.

But then a burst of icy magic shot past his ear and smashed into the troll's shoulder. Another howl echoed through the chasm. Ice began crawling across its shoulder and arm like creeping vines. Two more icy blasts hit the creature in the foot. First, one arm dropped when the ice solidified the appendage like stone. And then its leg dangled uselessly. Finally, the ice crept up its neck, its unforgiving tusks, and covered its bloodied, furry head.

The troll let go, and a sudden weight released his leg as it tumbled downward, hitting the icy chasm walls along the way.

Boom!

After what seemed to be an unending echo below, an eerie stillness filled the silence. Frosty wind whipped through his hair. The chasm's chill climbed his injured foot with promises of a slow, torturous death.

But the one thing he didn't hear…

"Lorella!" he gasped as he untangled his leg from ropes and broken planks, desperation in every action.

No answer.

Grimacing at the pain in his foot, he tucked his ax into his belt and began the arduous climb to the cliff's edge. His lungs burned with the effort of dragging himself over the lip of the chasm and into a pile of soft, frigid snow. For a moment, the cold eased some of his aches and pains, but he pushed himself to his hands and knees and frantically searched the area for blonde hair and silver wings.

Silence.

Snow, trees, and the chasm. Nothing more. Even the animals had run in fear of the troll.

Horror clung to him like smoke from a forest blaze. Choking and suffocating and devastating. Had she fallen into the chasm? Without much use of her wings, she wouldn't have survived.

His fingers carefully sifted through the snow as he looked for the small faerie when his search for her larger form yielded no results. He combed through soft powder near the edge of the chasm and ventured farther away until his fingers became numb enough to lose all feeling.

He continued his search.

At last, his hand brushed against something solid. He carefully wiped the snow away to reveal Lorella lying within the confines of the cold powder, her body limp and her eyes closed.

Dread pulsed through him as he nudged her shoulder with the tip of his finger, and then her side.

She didn't move.

"Please, no," he whispered.

Somewhere along their short journey, he had come to care for her. She was beautiful and brave and kind.

And her aid may have cost Lorella her life.

As gently as possible, he scooped her into his hands along with a handful of snow, wanting to put as much distance between him and the chasm as possible. He hurried across the white expanse of winter and ducked into the forest. Only when he found a safe, snowy area did he set her down and cover her entire body and wings with snow, only leaving her tiny face uncovered.

Blood dripped down his leg and smeared the snow, but despite his pain, he paced and paced some more within the confines of the clearing. He stooped down and pressed his ear just over her face, relieved to hear her small breaths escape her mouth.

She was alive.

So he paced some more. He wasn't sure if he had demanded her help or if she had given it freely. But he feared, no, he *knew* using her magic again would kill her. Especially when using her magic this time had rendered her unconscious.

He ran a hand over his mouth, torn as he glanced in the direction of his home. It wasn't far now. Just beyond the trees and down a large hill.

It wasn't supposed to end up like this… The faerie was supposed to heal his daughter and then fly free. But he had pushed her to the brink again and again. Now if she healed Rosamund, she would die. Either way, one of them wouldn't make it.

Tears trailed down his face as he stared up at the towering pine trees. They swayed in the breeze as if unaware of the turmoil inside his heart. And then he gazed down at Lorella's delicate frame. His heart ripped open, bleeding him dry. He collapsed to his knees, and fog escaped on his sigh.

"Forgive me," he whispered, his head bowed with shame. "I never meant to hurt or exhaust you. All I wanted was for my little girl to grow up into a young woman."

His entire body trembled with the weight of his decision. "I release you from my captivity. You are free."

With gentle fingers, he tucked the snow more securely around her with the finality of goodbye. Next, he located a reed of grass and sat with his back against a tree.

For hours, he blew on the reed to mimic the sound of a dying rabbit. Afternoon fell into dusk with no results. His head dipped forward as he began to nod off, but he snapped it up again when he heard a faint tinkle.

He searched the boughs above him but spotted nothing. However, he knew he'd heard it.

Setting down the reed, he spoke to the air. "I know you are there, faerie. Lorella is hurt. I don't know how to care for her. Please help me."

Another tinkle from somewhere above him.

And then silence.

Wincing, he climbed to his feet and backed away from Lorella with hands outstretched to show he meant no harm.

After several broken heartbeats, a shimmer of light darted down from the trees toward Lorella, and in the blink of an eye, they were both gone.

A heavy ache settled in his chest as he picked up his ax, buttoned his coat to the neck, and limped his way toward home. Every footfall sent a wave of agony from his leg to his heart. He was going to lose Rosamund. He would never see Lorella again. And life would never be the same. He'd already lost his wife. Losing his daughter would be the death of him. His heart wouldn't be able to handle the loss.

By the time night fell, he reached home. Light flickered through the window. Soft, curling smoke escaped the chimney and drifted toward melancholy stars. Silver. Bright. They reminded him of Lorella. How was she faring?

He released a long, foggy breath and swallowed his rising emotions. Little time remained for Rosamund, and he wanted to be a good father until the very dreary end.

After shaking the snow off his coat and stamping his boots on the porch, he opened the door, only to be greeted by flickering flames from the hearth and his dear, whimpering daughter lying on a cot near the fire.

"Papa!" Elaine cried as she rounded the corner and flew into his arms. "You've been gone for so long, I worried something happened to you. Did you capture the faerie?"

He busied himself by taking off his coat and shoes to give him a few moments to answer. "I did."

"Where is it?"

"I let her go."

"Oh." Elaine's lip quivered, but she said nothing more as she returned to Rosamund's bedside. "What happened to your leg?"

Pain rippled from his foot to his hip as he knelt beside Rosamund and smoothed back her brown hair damp with perspiration. "Just a little trouble on the road. Nothing a little salve can't help."

Rosamund shifted beneath his touch but didn't open her eyes. Her head blazed like hot coals. Her pale skin lacked life and luster. Each breath escaped as a rasp. Undoubtedly, Death stood just outside the door, waiting to come in.

"Go rest, Elaine," he said quietly as he dipped a cloth into a wooden bucket filled with icy water. "You've done so much for your sister already. Thank you."

Elaine kissed him on the cheek before drifting off to the room she usually shared with Rosamund. Only when she disappeared did his shoulders sag in defeat.

And quietly so his daughter wouldn't hear, he wept.

LORELLA'S EYELIDS FLUTTERED open, only to be met by a stream of silver moonlight. It caressed her face and filled her wings with cooling relief. The previously empty well of magic had filled while she slept, teeming with strength and endless possibilities.

She squeezed her eyes shut and opened them again to find herself at her sister's home, a small house built into the branches of a tree. The bed was made of twigs and blankets of woven leaves. A torch bug, Cassia's pet, flickered its light in the corner of the room where it dozed. A closet made of bark housed several beautiful gowns her sister had sewn all on her own. A rug lay in the middle of the house, the feathery down of bluebirds strewn together.

The tree bark door opened and closed, and Cassia flew inside with a bundle of snow, which she proceeded to spread across Lorella's feet.

"I'm happy to see you awake," Cassia said as she flitted across the room to better angle the windows to allow moonlight inside. "I was so scared I wouldn't find you in time."

Taking a deep breath of the moonlight, Lorella replied, "How did you find me?"

"When you didn't return home, I got worried and went out looking. I heard a distressed rabbit on my way, but it wasn't a rabbit." Her sister raised a single eyebrow.

Her heart thudded. Her eyes widened. And she shot into a sitting position, only to groan against the sudden movement. "You met Gabriel?"

"We didn't speak, but I saw him…and the way he looked at you." Cassia packed the snow tighter around her feet, all while a raging blush spread across Lorella's cheeks.

Continuing, her sister said, "I'll admit, he's handsome for a human. Though, not in the best shape. He was bloodied, and his eyes were red. You know, that kind of red humans get after crying a great deal."

She broke her feet out of the packed snow and leaped up, crossing the room in a single flit of wings. To her astonishment, her wings not only worked again, but they obeyed her. Cassia must have healed them with her own magic. "How long have I been unconscious?"

"Two days."

Two?!

The air rushed out of her lungs as if she'd been kicked. She placed her hand against the windowsill to steady herself. She remembered her almost kiss with Gabriel, the troll, and then using her magic to save him. Everything else was either blurry or black.

She realized with a start that she didn't feel the tug of compulsion to do whatever Gabriel might ask of her. It was gone. He had freed her.

A pit of dread formed in her stomach. Rosamund… Was she gone?

"They're not all the same," she finally whispered, still staring at the moon's glow. "Humans, they're not all the same. Gabriel is different."

Cassia smiled, now smoothing the wrinkles in the leaf blanket. "I never thought I'd hear you say those words. You've always been wary of humans. But Gabriel… You are fond of him, no?"

Her wings drooped as the pit of sadness grew larger within her belly. "Humans and faeries don't…intermingle."

Giving her a shrug, Cassia said, "I always say you are married to the moon. But perhaps a human is the next best thing. I won't tell our siblings if you don't want them to know. At least not yet."

Married to a human…

There were so many reasons it wasn't a good idea, but none of them mattered. Only Rosamund mattered. Tethered as a captive or not, she needed to heal the little girl.

If it wasn't already too late.

"I have to return. I don't know when I'll be back."

"Or *if*," her sister teased, but then her expression fell into bittersweet sadness. "Stay safe, Lorella."

"I will."

After kissing Cassia's cheek, she darted out the door. An urgency guided her wings as she hurried home to grab a few provisions and then shot through the dead of night with only the moon to guide her way. Two days. That was when she'd seen Gabriel last. It was two days too long. Not only had he managed to wedge himself into her heart and defy all her expectations of humans, but she cared for him and his two daughters she hadn't met.

Trees, snow, and frozen rivers passed by beneath her as she flew. Normally, she would bask leisurely in the moon-lit skies, but time was short. Rosamund needed her.

At the thought of the little girl, she flew faster. Even when exhaustion lay on the tips of her wings, she continued her trek through the skies. She flew over the chasm that had nearly claimed Gabriel's life. She whisked over the forest edges. She dashed toward the growing light of a human settlement.

Now, she flitted back and forth over the town, searching for a house a little way from the others and near the forest. Several met the description, and she glanced in each window. One home held an elderly couple sleeping in a bed. Another housed a woman who appeared to live by herself. Upon looking into the third home, her heart caught as she recognized the man inside.

Gabriel was hunched over in his chair, his head bowed. On a cot beside a hearth lay a frail girl. Perspiration dotted her entire pale face. Her chest rose up and down quickly as if struggling for breath.

Without waiting another moment, she transformed into her larger faerie form and wrapped a shawl over herself, mostly to obscure her wings and hair. She rapped softly on the door. When no one stirred within, she knocked a little louder.

The rumble of Gabriel's voice through the door sent shivers of excitement down her spine. But he didn't answer it. Instead, the door opened to reveal the face of a girl, her spirit aged far beyond her years.

"You must be Elaine," Lorella said as she extended a hand, and hesitantly, the girl shook it.

"Yes... Are you here for Papa? He asked me to send you away."

"Surely, he didn't mean *me*," she teased, her smile full of mirth. "I was under the impression that he liked me to some degree."

Elaine frowned, her eyebrows slanting into a deep furrow. "Who are you?"

"A faerie." She let her shawl slip to reveal a portion of her wing. "Will you invite me inside?"

The girl gasped, her eyes wide as she opened the door and stepped aside. Lorella entered cautiously, all while her eyes remained glued to Gabriel's back. By his lack of reaction, he hadn't heard the exchange just outside the door.

Gabriel ran a hand across his haggard face. "Elaine, please shut the door. The heat is escaping."

Swallowing her nervous energy, Lorella said, "But I work best in the cold."

He shot to his feet, his chair toppling backward as he spun around to face her. His hazel eyes widened into large spheres like pools of lush ferns. His mouth opened and closed several times as if at a loss for words.

Finally, he breathed, "You're here."

"I'm here." She crossed the remaining distance between them and squeezed his hand, but she only wished to throw her arms around his neck instead. Oh, how she'd missed him in their brief separation. "Of my own free will. I will see if something can be done for Rosamund."

Her shawl slipped off her shoulders to reveal her wings, and she handed it to Gabriel, who continued to gawk.

After righting the chair, she took a seat and placed her hand on top of Rosamund's head. The fever burned her fingers, desperate for relief. Her magic flowed through the girl's body, seeking out the source of the sickness.

The poor dear. She must be suffering greatly.

Rosamund leaned against her hand as if the small touch brought her immense relief. Almost as if she needed the comfort of…

A mother.

She glanced at Gabriel, who watched with trepidation in his expression, and told him, "I estimate only a few hours remain of her life. Her body stopped fighting and is now giving into the sickness."

He ran a hand over his face and pinched the bridge of his nose. "Can nothing be done?"

"That depends on what happens in the next hour. If her body takes my healing magic, she has a chance to survive this. But if it doesn't…"

"I understand. What can I do?"

Healing humans was a very different task than healing faeries. They needed warmth and sunlight. But she wanted, no *needed*, to try. "We must bring her fever down as I heal her. Gabriel, pick her up and place her in a bed of snow outside. The fire is certainly not helping to cool her down."

He immediately jumped into action as he cradled his daughter in his arms and moved her outside.

Lorella turned to Elaine next, handing her a pouch of herbs from her home, which should help Rosamund's body more easily accept the magic. "I need you to steep this in hot water and then cool it down as fast as you are able. Have your father help Rosamund drink it the moment it's cool."

The girl nodded profusely as she snatched the pouch and darted into another room.

Next, she found Gabriel outside, packing snow around Rosamund's little body. Lorella knelt beside the girl, placed her hands on either feverish temple, and closed her eyes as she concentrated.

Her magic escaped her fingertips and flowed into Rosamund. Her body drank it in hungrily as if dying of thirst, pulling on the conjoining thread of her magic for more. But Lorella fought back, only giving a steady stream of magic at a time. The healing process was meant to be slow and organized, not quick and careless.

Time passed in a haze. She was vaguely aware of Gabriel's presence beside her lifting Rosamund to help her drink the brewed tonic. But she never broke contact with her, and instead focused on channeling the healing magic into the girl, who continued to consume it with unending thirst.

Finally, her magic began to ebb as she gave as much as she could possibly give. And then she dropped her hands and opened her eyes. Her shoulders drooped. Her back ached. The faint shimmer of dawn approached the horizon.

"Lorella," Gabriel grunted as if waking from a light doze when he noticed her eyes open. He crouched over Rosamund and felt her forehead. No longer hot. Instead, her chest rose up and down with each peaceful breath. Her face no longer held beads of perspiration, pain absent in her expression.

He turned his attention to her, his eyes glassy. "It worked. You healed her."

"Perhaps not all the way." She trailed a strand of Rosamund's hair through her fingers, and again, the girl leaned into the touch. She smiled as a tenderness pricked at her heart. "If you will allow me to stay for a few days, I have more to give once I have some time to recover."

"You can stay forever if you'd like." His breath hitched as if surprised by his own words, his wide eyes mimicking her own. But before he said anything more, Rosamund shifted where she still lay in a patch of snow.

"Papa?" she croaked.

"I'm here, love. I'm here." He picked her up and disappeared inside the house, leaving Lorella staring after them while she continued to kneel in the snow. What had Gabriel meant? To stay forever as a captive faerie? Or as a wife?

Or perhaps he hadn't meant it at all.

She stood and flapped her wings to ease some of the knotted tension in her back, turning slowly to survey her surroundings. The cottage did indced lie secluded from the rest of the town, shaded by a variety of trees. Several plumes of smoke lifted into the skies from the direction of the town, and even from this distance, she heard townspeople stirring and beginning their day.

She rounded the house, only to jump in surprise when she spotted a large pen filled with a half-dozen cows and one goat. What kind of work did Gabriel do? She realized she didn't know a lot about him, but she also knew more than she ought to after their time together.

Gabriel was a good man.

"Why, hello there," she said as she tickled the goat beneath its scraggly chin. It bleated at her, and she responded with a laugh. A faint tinkle sounded in the laugh like music in the breeze.

"I've never heard your laughter before," Gabriel said, and she turned to find him leaning against the side of the house, staring with awe in his eyes. She blushed at the tenderness in his voice. "It's beautiful."

"Thank you," she murmured, lowering her gaze until her eyelashes shadowed her vision. "I do love animals, though they are much smaller when I'm in this form. I'm not quite used to it."

In just a few strides, he closed the distance between them, and she craned her neck to look up at him. He was so *tall*. And handsome. And when he touched her face with the back of his fingers, he stole the breath straight from her lungs.

His throat moved up and down as he swallowed. "It's been a long week. The children are both asleep." A pause. "You have no idea what you have done for me. Thank you, Lorella. I owe you everything. Name your price and it's yours."

Price…

She didn't like that word.

"What I have given comes without a price. I don't have children, but by the way you speak of your daughters, you clearly love them. And…for some strange, deranged reason," she grinned teasingly, "I have come to care about you. And your children. I would never have forgiven myself if I hadn't at least tried to help."

His throat bobbed with another swallow, and his fingers brushed her neck and threaded through her hair. He moved forward as if to kiss her. Every fiber of her being thrummed alive. Her heart jumped into a crazed rhythm.

And then fell when he squeezed his eyes shut and leaned away.

"Sorry." His murmured words escaped on his breath. "It's getting harder and harder to restrain myself. It's not fair for me to take—"

She stood on her toes and interrupted him with a brief kiss to his lips. When she pulled away, she watched his startled eyes grow wide, as well as the shimmer on his mouth sparkle beneath the rising sun. The shimmery blessing seeped into him and disappeared only moments later.

This time, he didn't hesitate or draw back. He cupped her behind the neck with one hand and the other pulled her closer by the waist. Their lips met in a gentle passion, hot enough to melt the snow off the face of the earth but cold enough to stir up a frenzied blizzard.

Her hands traveled up his chest, over his shoulders, and she tangled her fingers into his hair. A happy warmth spread through her body, a desire for more than just a wonderful memory. She wanted much more. A future with an abundance of kisses and each day filled with laughter and happiness.

"I was so scared I would never see you again," Gabriel murmured against her lips between kisses.

She smiled against his lips and pulled him closer until no space remained between them. "I never wanted to leave in the first place."

Finally, they broke apart, but not far when neither of them seemed to want to let go. He released a breath filled with disbelief. "But I captured you. I injured you. I stole you from your home and put your life at risk."

With a gentle movement, she placed her hand against his chest, just over his rapidly beating heart. "You healed me. You brought me laughter and happiness. You gave me a sense of purpose. You gave me hope for the future." She shook her head. "All the things you did were for a noble cause. And you never intentionally injured me."

"But…" A shuddering breath escaped him as he placed his large hands over hers. "At the chasm. It was my fault you used too much magic."

She laughed, another tinkle escaping on her breath. "You asked for nothing. You only called my name. And it was up to me to interpret your plea as I wished." She tipped her head to the side and smiled. "It was my choice to help you, to save you from that troll. That was *me*. Because I came to realize that my world would be a darker place without you in it."

"I could have lost you."

"And I would have lost you if I had done nothing."

A sneeze sounded beside one of the windows of the house, and both their heads darted in that direction to find the briefest flash of movement disappear behind the curtain.

"Well, I thought Elaine was sleeping," Gabriel said with a deep chuckle and twinkling eyes. "She was asking about you as I put her to bed. She wanted to know if you planned to stay." He gave her hand a squeeze. "*I* wanted to know if you would stay."

Lorella's heart picked up with nervous anticipation, and her cheeks flushed with heat. "For how long?" she whispered.

Another deep breath, and she could almost sense his nerves rolling off him in tune with hers. "Like I said before, forever, if you would have me."

She swallowed. "As a captive? Or..." She bit her lip, hardly daring to utter the words. But she wanted to know. *Needed* to know. "Or as your wife?"

"I think you know the answer already."

Yes, she did. But... "I would like to hear you say it."

Gabriel cradled her face with gentle hands, and she couldn't help but lean into his touch. "As my *wife*," he replied fervently. "I don't know the slightest thing about marrying a faerie. I'm not sure I'm even worthy of you. But this is what I want. Not just for my daughters but for myself. And if you're not ready, well..." His mouth lifted at the corners. "I want whatever you will give me."

Placing her hands over his, she said, "I want all of it. You. Your daughters. These mysterious cows."

He laughed and rested his forehead against hers. "I'm a dairy farmer. I made my living from milk and cheese."

"And magical remedies."

"Yes, and that, too."

A sigh escaped her as he kissed each corner of her mouth, her cheek, her jaw. She never wanted it to end.

"Stay," he begged in a whisper.

She turned her head to capture his mouth in another electrifying kiss that spread joy from her fingertips to her toes. "I would like that more than anything."

He lifted her by the waist and spun her as she giggled. Their joy and relief mingled together in another kiss. And when his laughter joined her own, she realized she loved the sound of it. Immensely.

As a human and a faerie, this marriage wouldn't be conventional, and perhaps it would be fraught with trials. But if she wasn't to be married to the moon…

A soft smile pulled on her lips as she gazed at Gabriel's handsome, untroubled face.

She supposed this was the next best thing.

ABOUT THE AUTHOR

Sydney Winward is an award-winning fantasy and paranormal romance author who dabbles in the occasional historical fiction. She loves building complex worlds filled with magic, strong characters, and emotional stories.

Sydney is the author of the Sunlight and Shadows Series and the best-selling Bloodborn Series, and when she's not writing, she's reading, thinking about stories, or going on adventures with her children. She lives in Utah with her husband and three amazing kids.

www.sydneywinward.com